Humpty Dumpty

Illustrated by Stuart Trotter

Humpty Dumpty sat on a wall.

Humpty Dumpty had a great fall.

All the King's horses

and all the King's men,

couldn't put Humpty together again.

Humpty Dumpty

Humpty Dumpty sat on a wall.
Humpty Dumpty had a great fall.
All the King's horses
and all the King's men,
couldn't put Humpty together again.